VALENTINE'S DAY
JITTERS

VALENTINE'S DAY
JITTERS

JULIE DANNEBERG

ILLUSTRATED BY JUDY LOVE

ini Charlesbridge

To Emmy and Zoey, my special little Valentines—J. D.

In memory of my mother and her jitters-provoking
Valentine's Day traditions, with love—J. L.

Published by Charlesbridge
9 Galen Street
Watertown, MA 02472
(617) 926-0329
www.charlesbridge.com

Library of Congress Cataloging-in-Publication Data
Names: Danneberg, Julie, 1958– author. | Love, Judith DuFour, illustrator.
Title: Valentine's Day jitters / Julie Danneberg; illustrated by Judy Love.
Description: Watertown, MA: Charlesbridge Publishing, [2021] | Audience: Ages 6–9. |
   Audience: Grades 2–3. | Summary: "Sarah Jane Hartwell has the jitters again as she
   tries to orchestrate an extra-special Valentine's Day party for her students; things may
   not go as planned, but her students know how much she cares and show her that they
   do too."—Provided by publisher.
Identifiers: LCCN 2020026650 (print) | LCCN 2020026651 (ebook) |
   ISBN 9781623541583 (hardcover) | ISBN 9781632899392 (ebook)
Subjects: CYAC: Valentine's Day—Fiction. | Teachers—Fiction. | Schools—Fiction.
Classification: LCC PZ7.D2327 Val 2021 (print) | LCC PZ7.D2327 (ebook) |
DDC [E]—dc23
LC record available at https://lccn.loc.gov/2020026650
LC ebook record available at https://lccn.loc.gov/2020026651

Printed in China
(hc) 10 9 8 7 6 5 4 3 2 1

Illustrations done in watercolor, transparent dyes, and India ink
   on Strathmore paper
Display type set in Lunchbox by Kimmy Designs
Text type set in Electra by Adobe Systems Incorporated
Color separations by Colourscan Print Co Pte Ltd, Singapore
Printed by 1010 Printing International Limited in Huizhou,
   Guangdong, China
Production supervision by Jennifer Most Delaney
Designed by Diane M. Earley

Valentine's Day was just around the corner, and Mrs. Hartwell had the jitters. She was busy planning the class Valentine's Day party, and she wanted it to be extra special, just like her students.

Remembering some of her party-planning issues in the past, Mrs. Hartwell decided to ask her room full of experts for advice.

During reading, between helping Emmy with a Band-Aid and searching with Jeff to find a just-right reading book, she asked students for suggestions on Valentine's Day craft projects. There was a consensus on glitter, glue, ribbons, and lace.

After math class, Mrs. Hartwell high-fived
Alexandra for knowing her math facts and gave
Jack a sticker for not giving up on his. Then she
asked the class for party-game recommendations.
Her students had lots of ideas.

Some she could use.

Some she couldn't.

As everyone lined up for recess, Mrs. Hartwell tied Andy's shoelace and reminded Sergio and Olivia to get their coats. Then she asked the students for advice on the perfect party treat.

"Cake!"
"With extra frosting!"
"And lots of sprinkles!"

The night before Valentine's Day, Mrs. Hartwell worked hard to get everything ready for the party. The cake took a lot of time. It was very complicated.

The next day, during lunch and recess, she bustled about, setting up the craft and the games.

"Can we see the cake?" the students asked when they came in, excited for another one of Mrs. Hartwell's parties.

"It's going to be a surprise!" she told them.

That afternoon, the students handed out their Valentine's Day cards. Then Mrs. Hartwell got them started on the craft project. There was glitter, glue, ribbons, and lace.

It turned out a little bit messier than Mrs. Hartwell expected.

"Oh my!" she said.

Next up, games!

Laughter rang out as students played pin-the-smile-on-the-teacher, bean bag heart toss, and candy heart bingo.

It was a bit livelier than
Mrs. Hartwell expected.
"Oh dear!" she said.

Finally, it was time for her extra-special cake surprise. Mrs. Hartwell couldn't wait. She knew it would be the perfect ending to a less-than-perfect party.

The students were definitely surprised.
"Is it supposed to look like that?" Jack whispered
to Maria.

"Ohhhh noooo!" wailed Mrs. Hartwell. "This party is a disaster! I wanted it to be extra special. I wanted to show you how much I care."

For a minute the students looked confused. Then they laughed. "But you show us that every day," they said.

"Silly Mrs. Hartwell," said Alexandra, patting her on the back.

The students decided to take charge.
Some of them helped Mrs. Hartwell clean the
frosting out of her hair and the glue off her shoes.
Sort of.

Some of them raced to clean up the mess.
Sort of.

And some of them fixed the cake.
Sort of.

But all of them took turns working on an impromptu valentine for Mrs. Hartwell. They wanted it to be extra special to show her how much they cared.

Once again, the classroom rang with laughter.

At the end of the day, the students gave Mrs. Hartwell their creation. "Happy Valentine's Day!" they cheered.

Mrs. Hartwell smiled. "It's perfect," she said.
"Just like you!" Emmy said.
Everyone agreed it was the best Valentine's Day party ever . . .